JUST DO YOU

AND KEEP YOUR EYE ON THE PRIZE

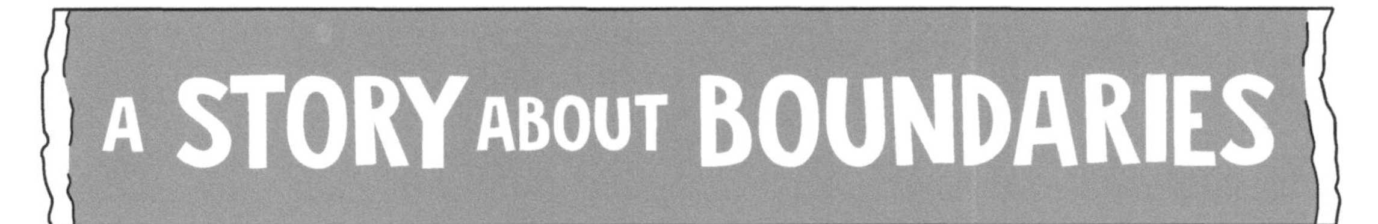

WORDS BY
BARBARA ESHAM

PICTURES BY
MIKE GORDON

sourcebooks
eXplore

It was the year my class was allowed to participate in the Morecaster School Science Fair.

I was so excited! Not only could we choose our very own topic, but also we each had a chance to win the prize for...

"MOST INTERESTING SCIENCE PROJECT."

It was going to be a challenge though.
Some of the projects were pretty complicated.

I wondered exactly how much help I would need for the project.

Sometimes my mom got so excited about my school projects that she helped too much.

But there was one thing I was certain of—this science project was going to be 100% my work.

Or maybe 93% my work, but no less!

I set up my own private work area
in the basement of our home.

It didn't take long to realize that the
project was too much for my parents to
resist. They wanted to "help."

We needed to create some
boundaries...

I worked on my project for weeks.

Mary, my older sister, didn't understand why
I would not allow Mom and Dad to help.

"You'll never get to play
on the weekends if you don't
let them help you, Dylan," she said,
looking up from her magazine—the Tonis Brothers Special
Edition, including bonus pictures of course.

MARY REALLY LOVED THE TONIS BROTHERS.

Don't get the wrong idea.

I loved to play outside, and sometimes I even avoided the occasional assignment until the last minute...

But for some reason, the science fair project was all that I could think about.

I worked for **WEEKS.**

I was dedicated to every little detail.

Some of my classmates completed their projects early and brought them to school before the due date.

I tried really hard not to let the other projects make me feel discouraged.

It was difficult for me not to compare my project with my classmates' projects, but I tried to keep my mind on what I was doing.

Lucky for me, Dr. Swarthmore, the science fair director and our school district's science coordinator, valued every student's hard work.

I knew she would notice the time and effort that each student put into their project.

The **BIG** day finally arrived!

The Morecaster School Annual Science Fair was one of the biggest events of the school year.

The auditorium was packed with teachers, parents, students, and even reporters from our town's local newspaper and television station.

I was careful to keep my project safe from the stampede.

I made sure to push it back just a little so it wouldn't get knocked over.

My sister and her friends were very interested in Christopher Sampson's project. Everyone in my sister's class thought Christopher looked just like Joe Tonis.

I guess he did...a little.

I felt proud explaining my science project to everyone who stopped by to see it.

It didn't matter to me if it wasn't the most interesting or exciting project. I was proud of it, and I didn't need to compare.

The day was filled with interesting ideas and exciting projects!

David Sheldon created the largest volcano in science fair history.

His parents had to hire a moving company to bring it in through the delivery entrance.

Katie developed a new spelling system to prove how difficult learning to spell and read can be.

Even the reading teachers from Morecaster Elementary were having a difficult time...

The entire auditorium fell silent when Dr. Swarthmore's voice came over the speaker. "Today has been very exciting for the science committee," she said with a smile.

"I see many future scientists and innovators in our auditorium, along with many unique and interesting projects," she added.

"After much thought and consideration, the science fair committee has decided to recognize the student who best reflects the work ethic of one of history's most famous scientists, Thomas Edison," Dr. Swarthmore announced. "Thomas Edison found happiness and reward in his work without focusing on the final outcome," she added.

"I find my greatest pleasure, and so my reward, in the work that precedes what the world calls success."—Thomas Edison

"It is with great pride that we honor Dylan Cooper with this year's Morecaster Science Fair first place prize," Dr. Swarthmore announced.

I almost didn't hear Dr. Swarthmore announce my name.

I was listening of course, but one of my jars tipped over, and I was trying to fix it.

"Congratulations, Dylan, you and Thomas Edison would have had much in common," she whispered as she placed the award in my hands.

Once the Science Fair was over, I carefully packed up my stuff. I had a feeling I would remember that day.

I would definitely remember the days leading up to it! I can't wait until next year's science fair. I'm already thinking of a new project!

But next year, I'm going to see if my grandparents can help keep my parents busy while I work.

The travel program on television claims, "It's the perfect month for a Caribbean cruise!"

A NOTE TO CARING ADULTS

FROM DR. EDWARD HALLOWELL

New York Times national bestseller, former Harvard Medical School instructor, and current director of the Hallowell Center for Cognitive and Emotional Health

Fear is the great disabler. Fear is what keeps children from realizing their potential. It needs to be replaced with a feeling of I-know-I-can-make-progress-if-I-keep-trying-and-boy-do-I-ever-want-to-do-that!

One of the great goals of parents, teachers, and coaches should be to find areas in which a child might experience mastery, then make it possible for the child to feel this potent sensation. The feeling of mastery transforms a child from a reluctant, fearful learner into a self-motivated player. The mistake that parents, teachers, and coaches often make is that they demand mastery rather than lead children to it by helping them overcome the fear of failure. The best parents are great teachers. My definition of a great teacher is a person who can lead another person to mastery.

ARE YOU AN EVERYDAY GENIUS TOO?

Everyday geniuses are **creative,** STRONG, **thoughtful,**
and sometimes learn a little differently from others.
And that's what makes them so special!

In *Just Do You and Keep Your Eye on the Prize*, Dylan is determined to complete his science project without too much help from his parents. Getting extra help can be a good thing, but sometimes it feels even better to accomplish something on your own.

Have you ever felt like someone was helping you more than you wanted them to? Or that someone was taking over something you were trying to do on your own?

What happened?

Dylan set up his own work area in his basement to keep his parents away from his science project. He says he needed to create some boundaries. Boundaries are ways to set limits. You can think of boundaries like a fence around a person's yard. You can do this by creating real physical boundaries—like Dylan does by creating a space in his basement to work. Or you can do this with verbal, or spoken, boundaries—like directly telling others what you want them to do or not do.

Here are a few other things you can try:

- Talk it out. Sometimes it's best to just say what you mean directly to the person. For example, "Thanks for offering to help, but I would like to do this myself."
- Give helpers specific tasks. If you do want your mom's help, but you don't want her to take over, tell her exactly what you are ok with her doing.
- Set goals for your work.
- Practice makes you better. The more you work at something on your own, the less help you'll need.

It's ok to make mistakes as long as you grow from them. Sometimes we are afraid to try things on our own because we are afraid we might fail. But making mistakes is one of the best ways to learn how we can get better at the thing we're trying to do. What are some other ways you can keep your eye on the prize?

Remember, everyday geniuses are creative, strong, thoughtful, and sometimes learn a little differently from others. It's never a bad thing to be different—embracing and learning from our differences is what makes the world a better place!

ABOUT THE AUTHOR

Author Barbara Esham was one of those kids who couldn't resist performing a pressure test on a pudding cup. She has always been a "free association" thinker, finding life far more interesting while in a state of abstract thought. Barbara lives on the East Coast with her three daughters. Together, in Piagetian fashion, they have explored the ideas and theories behind the definitions of intelligence, creativity, learning, and success. Barb researches and writes from her home office in the spare time available between car pools, homework, and bedtime.

ABOUT THE ILLUSTRATOR

Cartooning has brought Mike Gordon acclaim in worldwide competitions, adding to his international reputation as a top humorous illustrator. Since 1993 he has continued his successful career based in California, gaining a nomination in the prestigious National Cartoonist Society Awards. Mike is the renowned illustrator for the wildly popular book series beginning with *Do Princesses Wear Hiking Boots?*

Cover design by Travis Hasenour

The story text was set in OpenDyslexic, a font specifically designed for readability with dyslexia.
The back matter was set in Adobe Garamond Pro.

Published by Sourcebooks eXplore, an imprint of Sourcebooks Kids
P.O. Box 4410, Naperville, Illinois 60567-4410
(630) 961-3900
sourcebookskids.com
Originally published as *Keep Your Eye on the Prize* in 2014 in the United States of America by Mainstream Connections Publishing.
This edition issued based on the hardcover edition published in 2018 in the United States of America by Sourcebooks Kids.
Cataloging-in-Publication Data is on file with the Library of Congress.

Source of Production: Lightning Source, Inc., La Vergne, TN, USA
Date of Production: May 2024
Run Number: 5040834

Printed and bound in the United States of America.
LSI 10 9 8 7 6 5 4 3 2 1

Printed in the USA
CPSIA information can be obtained
at www.ICGtesting.com
CBHW040326220424
7192CB00001B/4